MARC BROWN

ARTHUR'S COMPUTER DISASTER

RED FOX

For
Eliza Morgan Brown

A Red Fox Book

Published by Random House Children's Books
20 Vauxhall Bridge Road, London SW1V 2SA

A division of Random House UK Ltd
London Melbourne Sydney Auckland
Johannesburg and agencies throughout the world

5 7 9 10 8 6 4

First published in the United States of America by
Little, Brown & Company and simultaneously in Canada by
Little, Brown & Company (Canada) Ltd 1997

First published in Great Britain by Red Fox 1998

Printed in Hong Kong

RANDOM HOUSE UK Limited Reg. No. 954009

ISBN 0 09 926577 X

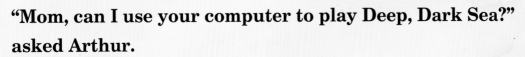

"Mom, can I use your computer to play Deep, Dark Sea?"
asked Arthur.

"What's Deep, Dark Sea?" asked D.W.

"Only the greatest game in the universe," said Arthur.

"Can I, Mom, please?"

"What's the game about?" asked D.W.
"A haunted sunken ship," said Arthur.
"With skeletons, ghosts, and sharks."
"Sounds spooky," said D.W.

"Mom, please," begged Arthur.

"Oh, all right," said Mother, "but finish your dinner first."

Arthur finished his dinner in a jiffy.

Once Arthur started playing Deep, Dark Sea,
he couldn't stop.
"Time for bed," said Father.
"But Dad, I've almost found *the thing*," said Arthur.

"When I find *the thing*, I can win stuff."

"You can find *the thing* tomorrow," said Father.

"It's bedtime."

"I'm ready for bed," said D.W. sweetly.

The next morning, Buster came over to play
Deep, Dark Sea.
"Sorry, boys," said Mother. "I'm really busy.
I need my computer all day."

Just then the phone rang. It was for Mother.
"I have to run to the office," she said. "Now don't touch
my computer."

After Mother had left, Arthur and Buster stared at
the computer.

"I know what you're thinking," said D.W.

"But I'm so close to finding *the thing*," said Arthur.

"You could probably find it before your mom gets home,"
said Buster.

"I'm telling Dad," warned D.W.

"I'll give you my desserts for a whole week," said Arthur.

"And play doll's house with me whenever I say so?"
asked D.W.

"Yes," grumbled Arthur.

"And call me Your Royal Highness . . . ?" asked D.W.

"Don't push it," said Arthur.

Arthur loaded up the game.

"Look out for the Squid Squad!" yelled Buster.

"I'm running out of oxygen," said Arthur.

"Look," said Buster. "A treasure chest!"

"That's it!" screamed Arthur. "That's *the thing*! I've found it!"

"Let me open it!" shouted Buster.

"I found it," argued Arthur.

They both dived for the mouse.

The keyboard crashed to the floor.
"Uh-oh," said Arthur.
"You're in big trouble," said D.W.

Just then the phone rang. Everyone jumped.

It was Mother.

"I won't be home until tonight," she said. "Everything all right?"

"Umm, fine, just great," said Arthur.

"You know, Mom can tell when you're lying," whispered D.W.

"Maybe we can fix it before she gets home," said Arthur.

Arthur looked through the computer manual.
"There's nothing in here about Deep, Dark Sea accidents,"
he said.
"Are you sure you've got the right manual?" asked D.W.

"The Brain can fix anything," said Buster. "Let's ask him."
"Alan's not home," said the Brain's mother.

They checked the library.

They checked the museum.
Just when they were about to give up, they found him.

"Are you doing a science experiment?" asked Buster.
"No, I'm skipping stones," said the Brain. "It's fun!"

Everyone went back to Arthur's house.
The Brain examined the computer.
"Hmmm," said the Brain. He shook his head.
"That bad?" asked Arthur.
"It must be," said the Brain. "I can't find the problem."
"Well, thanks for trying," said Arthur.
"Now you're in really, really big trouble," said D.W.
"If the Brain can't fix it, who can?" said Buster.
"I have an idea," said Arthur.

Arthur explained his problem to the computer expert.
Then the computer expert explained how much it would
cost to repair.
"That's more birthday money than I'll ever see in my
whole life," said Arthur. "I'm doomed."

We're all doomed," said D.W. "Because now Mommy will lose her job and we won't be able to keep our house and we'll all have to live in the cold on the street and we'll all get ammonia and probably die and it's all your fault, Arthur!"

That evening, Arthur hardly touched his dinner.

"Hi, I'm home," called Mother.

"Mom, how about a game of cards?" asked Arthur.

"And a family bike ride?"

"Don't have time, sweetie," said Mother. "I have tons of work to do."
Mother headed for the computer.
Arthur felt sick.

Arthur ran after Mother.
D.W. ran after Arthur.
Buster ran home.

Just as Mother's finger was about to hit the ON button,
Arthur yelled, "Stop!"
"I was playing Deep, Dark Sea, and the screen went blank.
I'm sorry. I've wrecked it. It's all my fault."

"That happens to me all the time," said Mother.
"Did you jiggle the switch?"
Mother jiggled the switch, and the game came on.
"Why didn't you call me?" asked Mother.
"Always call me with your problems."
"I thought you'd be cross," said Arthur.
"I'm not cross," said Mother. "I'm disappointed."

"Am I going to be punished?" asked Arthur.

"Of course," said Mother. "You did something you weren't supposed to do."

"Make the punishment really good," said D.W.

"No computer games for a week," said Mother. "Now, get ready for bed. I'll be up to say good night in a few minutes."

Arthur and D.W. did as they were told.
Then they waited for what seemed like a very long time.
"Mom," called Arthur. "Time to tuck us in."

"In a minute," said Mother. "The sharks are attacking!"
"Maybe we should tuck ourselves in tonight," said D.W.
"Good idea," said Arthur.

"I'll be right up," called Mother. "As soon as I blast these skeletons from the treasure chest."

"Good night, Mom," called D.W.
"Good night, Mom," called Arthur.